The Meadow

Doris Rowland Thompson

E dom

happy reading

ms Dares

11 - 27 - 13

VANTAGE PRESS
New York

Illustrated by Tanya Stewart

FIRST EDITION

Copyright © 2006 by Doris Rowland Thompson

Published by Vantage Press, Inc.
419 Park Ave. South, New York, NY 10016

Manufactured in the United States of America
ISBN: 0-533-15243-7

Library of Congress Catalog Card No.: 2005904425

0 9 8 7 6 5 4 3 2 1

To Tristan, Brandon, Elizabeth, and Tyler

Tribute to Mr. Guy Nichals

I would like to pay tribute to Mr. Nichals, principal of Fredonia High School, Fredonia, Kentucky (1940s). He will never know how he affected my life. He was my mentor and the best school teacher any young student could possibly ever know. I lived for his sociology classes. They were educational and exciting. His humor and wit made his teaching a lot of fun. He taught the science of origin and functioning of human society, the fundamental laws of social relations. Mr. Nichals had the unique ability of making one feel worthy and smart. "All things are ready, if our minds be so" (Shakespeare). His love for Browning, Longfellow, and Shakespeare opened up a world for a lot of students they had never heard or dreamed about. I will forever remember and thank him.

—Doris Rowland Thompson

The farmhouse is small compared to the big barn across the road, in the field where the farm animals lived, ate, and slept at night. Behind the barn is the meadow where the cows spend their days grazing on clover and chewing their cud.

Many species of birds live alongside the cows. There is a particular old blackbird, called Blackie, who has spent a lot of summers in the meadow. Blackie is ruler of the roost, with his *Konk La Reee* calls and red wing patch.

He has raised many healthy babies with his mate, the missus, and a dear old friend, a meadowlark, who was continually flying from milkweed to milkweed ruffling his throat feathers with his *See you See yeer* and rattling flight calls.

Blackie and Larky have been friends for many years. Both lost their mates earlier in life. They love to check out the young families that come to the meadow to raise their young and forage in the apple orchard in the next field, which has an abundance of insects and worms to feed the baby birds.

There are cardinals with their bright red feathers. They are especially anxious to see the "maskless" redbird, who is so timid he seems to be afraid of the other birds.

When the apple trees are in bloom, there is always a flutter of activity, when the ruby-throated hummingbirds are so busy buzzing from tree to tree all day long. It is enough to make Blackie and the Lark tired.

The nest in the old fencepost is already taken by a pair of bluebirds. They were happy they got there before the house sparrows. Blackie calls them the commoners. He loves the bluebird *Cherry Chur Lee* call. Bluebirds are becoming so rare, it is good they have come back to the meadow for another summer.

Along the meadow's edge there is a creek and woodland area where lots of birds build their nests every year near the water. The house wrens are in the old trees, with plenty of nesting sites made available by the pileated woodpecker feeding in the open woods on tree trunks. The creek is useful for both birds and cows. In both morning and afternoon, the cows come to the creek for a drink of water. On hot summer days they will walk and splash in the shallows. They also dodge the barn swallows that come to the creek's edge gathering mud to build and repair their nests.

Blackie loved all the colorful birds: the yellow warbler, bobbing his tail and his dark eyes, summer tanager, with his scarlet feathers, and yellow-gold finches, always gleaning on thistle bushes. Cows stayed away from the thistle!

One of Larky's favorites is the orchard oriole, with deep chestnut feathers. They help to protect the fruit on the trees from worms and caterpillars. When they arrive in spring, they go from tree to tree singing all day long. No day is complete without a rowdy visit of the grackles; they come in droves and can glean the entire area in a matter of seconds. The orchard sounds like a supermarket—and in a flash they are gone!

The farmhouse where the Burns family lived and raised their kids is a modest country home. They have three daughters, Marie, Molly, and Lilly, a four-year-old son, Frank, and his black dog, Sport. Then there are all the cats in the barn, to help keep the mice away from the cow feed. The Burns family is usually up early to milk the cows before school. When the chores are finished, the cows will be put out to pasture for the day.

In the early morning the birds are busy gathering food to feed their young and singing cheerful good morning songs.

To board the school bus on the highway, the young ladies will take a path through the meadow, crossing a bridge over the creek to the dirt road, which could be real muddy after a good rainfall.

The eldest daughter, Marie, always has time to check the meadow for anyone in need. She will scan the fields, trees, and bushes and has rescued many wounded birds. Blackie and Larky know of her love for all the animals and think her caring is amazing. They hope she will become an animal doctor, a veterinarian.

On the other hand, young Frank loved his dog, Sport, as well as all the birds. He would sit on the front porch for hours watching the robins cock their heads sideways, listening for earthworms in the front yard. Frank would let the girls know if any of the baby robins had fallen from their nests, and would safely tuck the birds away in the corner of the yard until the girls returned home from school.

School was very important for Marie, Molly, and Lilly, and each young lady did very well in her studies. Marie planned to be a veterinarian; Molly, a nurse; and Lilly just wanted to be a farmer's wife to raise corn and tobacco, and to milk cows.

When the girls returned home from school each day, taking the path through the meadow, it was time to check on the birds.

They are not surprised to find two mourning doves in the grassy field. Lilly loves their trim bodies and their mournful calls. The killdeer, Molly's favorite, with his silly long legs, is also common in the farm field. Its nest is found on the ground, usually around some stones. Like many birds, it will feign a broken wing or leg to lead intruders away from its nest.

Blackie and Larky know that later the cows will come to the gate and enter the barn lot for nighttime feeding and milking. After school, the farm seems to come alive with the children hurrying about, getting the chores done. Every night, stalls are cleaned and strawed, hay is put down for the cows, and all the troughs are filled with sweet feed.

After the feeding and milking is finished, all of the cats in the barn will get a saucer of fresh warm milk. Afterward, Lucy, a mama cat, will call her litter of four kittens to her side to clean their faces and paws.

Suppertime for the Burns family brings together Papa and Mama, their daughters and young son, Frank. It is time to share the events of the day. Mama Burns is the quiet one in the family and has plenty of time to listen to her children's stories while Papa Burns retires to the front porch with his pipe. He is soon taking a well-deserved nap.

Blackie and Larky make their final check before night falls on the meadow. The birds are seeking their nests. Fireflies are starting to light up and small animals are scurrying about in the open field.

Near the edge of the wooded area, a small screech owl parks by the wood lot. He has a good view of the orchard and open field, and, with quavering whistles ending in a pitch, he lets you know he will be looking for small rodents feeding nearby. A faint whip-poor-will's call can be heard in the distance.

The two old friends have had a long and busy day. Only the chirping of the insects can be heard in the stillness of the warm summer night.

Each day brings a new adventure. Today there is a big fuss at the farmhouse. Something is wrong with Sport. He keeps pawing at the side of his head and can't seem to swallow his food. In tears, Frank is calling for Marie, and she hurries to her young brother's side to examine his beloved pet. During the night, Sport has chased a gopher into a hole and while trying to dig out, he had bitten down on a root from a nearby tree that had broken off into the roof of his mouth.

By reaching inside, Marie had to clasp the root and pull as hard as her small body would allow. What a relief when the root came out and she happily dried up the tears on her brother's cheeks.

Keeping up with all of the birds, cows, and family pets is a full day for Blackie and the meadowlark. Blackie had come to depend more on the children to help check on the birds. One day, he spotted a Cooper's hawk, one of the biggest predators of songbirds, perched on a nearby telephone pole. Blackie was always sad to lose one that could sing so beautifully.

With one sweep of the meadow, the hawk could wipe out an entire family and leave the baby birds as orphans without someone to feed and care for them every day.

Everyone is on the alert and well aware of the hawk's potentially brutal attack. The only escape for the small birds is in the fencerow where the wild, thorny rose bushes grow.

Summer seems to get shorter every year and one cool night will start the leaves to turn. The birds must be ready to make the trip to a warmer place for the colder days ahead.

The meadowlark is concerned Blackie is not looking well. His plumage is dull and getting thin; his eyes are growing dim. The bond between the two friends is so strong that no words need be spoken. They know that their time together has been a long and valuable friendship. They hope Blackie will have the strength to fly farther south and they are making plans to leave soon. The sun is starting to rise. It is a Saturday morning and Larky is hoping for a quiet and peaceful day for making their plans, not the usual hustle and bustle of the weekday rush. Blackie is waiting in his favorite spot, on the old post by the orchard.

You could depend on him being there rain or shine, watching the young birds scuffling over the apples that had fallen from the trees during the night. They reminded him of his younger days. By the end of the summer they will be full grown and will return to the meadow in springtime for mating and raising families of their own.

Larky can see a flock of birds gathered around the old fence post. Blackie must be in trouble; perhaps a fight among the young birds. Sometimes they could be hard to manage, always so full of energy, but eager to be taught that family and friendship can be one of life's greatest treasures.

He found Blackie basking in the warm sunshine with his chest all puffed up, eyes alert, and looking like his old self.

The young birds were gathered around, listening to him. Larky knew how much pride Blackie had in teaching and planning for the migratory trip. Larky could feel the excitement building already.

With the summers getting shorter, in late August and early September the male hummingbird will be the first to leave. In fact, he has already left for Mexico.

Everyone is looking forward to the trip down south, with sunny days, a new supply of food, and meeting up with old friends. The date has been set for their last meeting. It will be in the maple tree near the Burns family's farmhouse.

All afternoon you can hear the birds chattering and singing (mostly starlings imitating other species of birds). Mr. Burns tells his family it is time, the birds will be leaving soon. Mrs. Burns smiles and winks at the children, knowing they have watched after and loved all the birds.

It has been a good summer—-not a single loss to the hawk or any other predator, and best of all, Blackie is healthy again.